Silent Voices, Loud Whispers

Silent Voices, Loud Whispers
by Ashee B Bansaal
Paperback Edition

First Published in 2023 in India by

Inkfeathers

Inkfeathers Publishing
Vivek Vihar, New Delhi 110095
www.inkfeathers.com

ISBN 978-81-19483-06-8

Silent Voices, Loud Whispers

Ashee B Bansaal

Inkfeathers Publishing
www.inkfeathers.com

I dedicate this book to the almighty, Shri Radhakrishna,
for giving me the strength to find the light.

A special dedication to my grandmother, Mrs. Babita Bansal,
the one that completes my name (middle name 'B'),
for always residing in my heart and giving me
the courage to endure.

(My Grandmother)

I thank my mother, Ms. Pallavi Bansal, my *massi* (maternal aunt)
Ms. Priyanka Bansal, my grandfather Mr. Naresh Bansal,
my aunt Ms. Meenu Sharma for always being there.
Well, what should I say?
They are the reason for the way I am today.
The real people behind all my success so far,
the pillars of my life, they mean the world to me.

I would like to thank my friend Avishi Sharma,
for bringing laughter into my life, listening to all my crap,
and standing up for me, come what may.

Contents

About the Author

Ashee B Bansaal is a remarkable young poet, known for her exceptional talent and passion for various artistic pursuits. A standout moment in her academic journey was her remarkable performance in the grade 10 CBSE boards, where she achieved an extraordinary score of 499 out of 500. Her insatiable curiosity and relentless pursuit of excellence have propelled her beyond the confines of academia, leading her to explore various artistic realms. Beyond her academic accomplishments, she possesses a multi-layered personality, reflecting her diverse talents and creative passions. Her poetry resonates with readers, evoking deep introspection and connecting with human experience on a profound level. In addition to her mastery of language, she is an avid flutist, enthralling audiences with her melodic tunes. With an artistic eye and a passion for visual storytelling, she is also an accomplished photographer and a Tanjore artist. One cannot truly understand her without acknowledging her deep religious faith. She is a devout believer in Shri Radhakrishna and draws inspiration from the profound teachings of the Shrimad Bhagwat Geeta. Her spirituality permeates her work, infusing it with a sense of purpose, compassion, and wisdom.

Author's Note

"Just remember, the world will always give you sweets of salt and chillies. Learn to make your own sweets of sugar."

The perspective of life that I have today (well it ought to change as I grow up) is how I define my life and myself. Not only has this life presented me with obstacles, right from being a single parent child and seeing my mother struggle to being tormented and sidelined by the students at school for just being a 'topper'. Well, for these obstacles, I thank the almighty, for I feel that these are the ones that I have chosen for myself. They are the ones who have made me what I am today. A life with ripples of challenges is what I prefer because at the end, it is these ripples that help you climb the highest of peaks by showing you the lowest of depths. These trials, some by fire and others by flower have inspired me to pen down my thoughts in the form of poetry.

So, I welcome all my readers to find their ripples in mine and feel the real power inside ourselves.

The Life

1. The Frail Silence

Some say that silence is the most fragile,

Some say that glass is,

For I claim that

Silence is the glass which

Is fragile

Which when breaks,

Does it shatter itself?

Or the ones around

Is the question that awakes.

2. The Prized Possession

Can you imagine?

My entire life

What I wanted

I had,

But what I thought I had

Is what I didn't have.

Can you imagine?

All throughout,

I thought I had the eyes

To see this world,

But in the end

Finally, I realized of the

Lack of this prized possession to see the real world.

Can you imagine?

Every day I yearned

For a better life,

But finally

Did I realize that the life I had

was in itself a luxurious possession.

3. Live in Yourself

Has mind ever led you
To this feeling new,
But old? Thinking of your
Identity and your
Goals in your life
Or just about 'life'.

The young Grey beards!
Don't you think to be winged?
Before making this dive
You should first take control of your thrive
And not let others, for you, to plan it out
Just don't forget, this life is about
How you treat yourself
And how much you live in yourself.

4. It Too Shall Pass

In deep trouble,
I recalled the one
Whom I had bid
An adieu for good
But then he said,
'Remember, it too shall pass.'

A grave battle when I won
I called the one
Who was very dear
And was always there to hear,
But then he said,
'Remember, it too shall pass.'
'It too shall pass.'

5. The Feeling of Fun

With thousands in our mind
And hundreds of puzzles to unwind,
So often do we forget
The most vital thing to get.

It's easy and difficult,
But definitely not unknown to the cult,
With so much stress
Why do we suppress?

The feeling and the need
Of having fun, indeed,
what we forget, In the life
Is the main reason to be alive.

6. The Only One

Well, to you,
I might be quiet.
Well, to someone,
I might be annoying
Well, to another,
I might be talented.
Well, to some others,
I might be totally unknown.
Well, to each in the world,
I might be different.
But to none but me
I will always be the only one.

7. The Ultimate Life's Truth

With the thought of amending my life's past,
Especially the times when I was distraught,
Well, I climbed onto the machine fast.
'My friend, take me to my past.'

While the route,
which seemed to just end,
I thought it to be the most precious fruit
Finally, in less than a minute,
I reached my destination
And felt as if my success had no limit,
For it was in my life, the father's contribution.

Oh! Happiness changed its way.
When I realized very fast
That it was the same day
When I had left, not the past

The excitement came to an end,

But the machine said, in contrast,

"Oh! My friend,

Why has your smile passed?

You've reached your destination at the end.

For 'today is your future's past.'"

8. The Luxury of Hope

The little ant
Asked the plant,
"Where is my home?"
To me, its location is now unknown.

He asked every single one,
But ignorance was the one
That he met
Even after he tried his best.

Just when he sat,
He felt that
Hope isn't a need,
But a luxury, indeed.
Luxury to endure the times challenging
With a smile never-ending.

Day and night,

He held his hope tight.

Searched his home

And crossed paths with an unknown.

It was that unknown,

Indeed, who helped him find his home.

But in the end,

He asked that friend,

"Where would I have been

If with me, you had not been?"

But she just said, "Don't worry,

You had the hope's luxury."

9. Two Pillars of Life

What does life depend on?
Have you brought this question to dawn?
Well, for me,
Only two words I see
On which depends our life
And for what we need not thrive.

Be it success or failure,
We must endure
Because of just two
Our friends and enemies, nothing new.

No, we need not go,
Somewhere, you know,
We need not even find
Someone that kind,
We just need to know
How to sow.

If we have in life
The patience to thrive
Then we need not
a friend, if carefully thought.

If we have in life
The anger at every strive
Then we need not
An enemy, if carefully thought.

10. The Real Success

In this world,
You will find
Even those whom you are fond of.
Even those whom you aren't fond of.
Even those whom you've hurt.
Even those who you have hurt

In your life,
You will have to thrive,
But in that process,
Don't forget to celebrate your ultimate success.
And what might that be?
Wondering you must be.
Your success isn't your grades
Or your material planes.
But instead, just your happiness
And in peril, your calmness.

11. The Perfect Sunrise

In the crowd,
I heard a sound
Shouting at me
Telling me not to be
So optimistic about the descend,
For he said, it is ultimately the end.

Well, I said
Everyone in their head
Need to seek it out
Whether to be crying
Pointlessly any reason
Or to be the perfect sunset in every season.

12. One Life, One Choice

What fate wrote for you is not important.

What did you do when you had a breath?

Always asked for two.

But I am sorry, dear.

Life is one!

Opportunity is one!

Choosing the bed of roses,

you always cursed your life.

But my dear, choice is given once.

Who remembers when you were born and when you died?

It was just a second's gap.

Napped your entire life!

But my dear, choice is given once.

13. A Life of a Soldier

Here comes the spring,
New leaves have stepped in.
Some are bold; some are timid.
The tree has a smile.
Everyone is in a rush
to see who the newborns are.

Next comes the summer.
Some have fled away, biding their families adieu
going to guard their forest.
Dead for the tree,
but soul for the forest.
Weeps the tree, smiles the tree
biding his child, a final adieu.
Giving away responsibility to the forest
Now, the leaf is not his but the forest.

Comes next, the autumn with the fall.
After a blue moon, came the leaf
wrapped in colours.
dead as he was,
had a smile on his face,
left the forest,
and went to heaven.

At last, comes the winter
with all sobbing and weeping.
The leaf sacrificed with happiness,
but see,
it's the tree and his mates who
have now sacrificed their happiness.

The leaf is immortal,
though dead
has his name on every tree.

Life's a season,

a bittersweet season.

Once you choose,

never think back.

Brave enough to be born

So, be brave enough to embrace death.

14. Identity

Who am I?

Am I just a child?

Or

Am I just a student?

You are an explorer in your life.

You are a fighter for yourself.

You are a seeker seeking knowledge.

Answered; someone seemed to be up in the clouds,

But actually

It was me, myself, my insight

Who

Teaches me the best,

Regulates my life,

not according to my fate,

not according to my comfort,

but according to my destiny, my life's platform.

How am I?

Will I be able to leave an imprint on the world?

Will the world remember me?

You are a star who can shine.

You have the will to change the world.

You can change the world.

You can give the world a lot it needs.

Answered the one who's my closest!

Every time I put forth these questions.

Comes teaching with these retorts,

"Those who invest their time properly

at any age, may it be,

will have the right to say,

'I have' rather than 'I could have'. "

15. The Key to the Real Life

Open your eyes,
But you are still blind.
Wonder why?
And
Think how?

You're always blind.
From spending your life to taking any decision,
From thinking to doing anything,
Your eyes are always wrapped,
Even your thoughts are bonded
In the shackles of fear.
You are always shaking.

This fictional wild imagination of yours
Changes you,
Writes your new personality
And makes a new coward you.

What are you afraid of?
Why are you afraid?
The answer is one and only one:
The fear of death haunts me,
Shakes,
Binds,
Not just you, but everyone in this small little world.

Death
What is your next experience,
Which can be any moment.
No idea why you are afraid of death.
Death is inevitable.
Death is what is natural.
So why be afraid of it?

Be fearless.

When no one can haunt you and shake you,

Then you will become the real you,

and only then,

you will come to know what this world is all about.

Fear is not the path

to be chosen.

Fearlessness is the first key to your real life.

16. Wedding

It's not about exchanging gems or stones.

It's about exchanging hearts.

It's not about selecting a venue.

It's about selecting a place in everyone's hearts.

It's not about new clothes.

It's about new relations.

It's not about the grief of separation.

It's about the content of unification.

It's not about the vows that will bind you.

It's about the love that will liberate you.

17. Life: A Path

Have the courage to choose it,
Have the will to face it,
For only one has life at the end
Out of the two
Before you.

Have the wisdom to choose it,
Have the faith to face it,
Both paths are dark in the beginning,
But only one with lighted life in the ending.

Have the strength to choose it,
Have the intellect to face it,
For one is a bed of rose bloom,
And the other is a bed of rose cane.

Have the mind to choose it,
Have the power to face it,
For only you will know
Which path leads to the light
and
Which to the dark.

Have the calm to choose it,
Have the vigour to face it,
For there is only one way
"To start from the start."
Jumping to the end
and
then choosing life's path
is not what life is.

18. My Identity

I don't know who I am.

I don't know why I am.

I don't know how I am.

I don't know where I am.

I don't know whose I am.

But

After my soul, my mind and my heart spoke together,

I know I am a power.

I know I am here to bring a change.

I know I am in high spirits as long as I wish to be.

I know I am in a world shackled in the chains of momentary wishes.

I know I am my own and this world's, which needs to be liberated.

19. The Fate's Ploy

Served on my plate,
Ripe fruits of fate
Considered it a treat
which with content did I eat.

Served on my plate,
Rotten fruits of fate
Thought from them, I could run away.
But, forced was I to eat,
For that possibility had faded away.

Served yet again on my plate,
Rotten fruits of fate
Surprised and bewildered, I thought,
"Have tried to escape but was caught
So, let's wait and see what it has brought."

With cold contempt did I eat,
But in glee, concluded it as a miraculous feat,
For they were the best fruits of the seat

At last, did this halfwit understand
The destiny's stand.
For it overrules
My every rules and regulations.
For there is no escape
which we can only embrace.

20. The Most Epic Battle

The most epic battle
Have I witnessed.
A warrior and a saviour
Have I emerged
With the greater power to identify
Which the epic battle was.
Here I stand,
Defying all odds and strands.

This battle,
This epic battle
I am talking about
No, this is no world war.
This is no civil war.

This is the war
that every human fights
inside his own self,
and the outcome serves
the answer to the side he will serve.

The crushing thoughts,
not the weapons,
lead us to hell
within ourselves.
It's painful,
but rewarding.
Always rewarding,
If not, fight for the reward.

21. God's True Grace

God's grace, are you.
My beloved diamond, are you.
A harbinger of smile on my face,
You truly are God's grace.
In fortune or plight,
In support or fight,
Knew my soul,
You'll always embrace me as a whole.
Forever in your debt shall I be,
But that's what I would like, believe me!
My supporter, My fighter,
My unique mother.

22. The Servant and the Master

Today are the plates served
Finally, after each trait is summoned
With the plate of felicity in her hand,
So diverse
Contented I felt
Crowned I felt
She ran towards me,
So, did I
I ate it all

The next hour
She came again
Delighted as I already was
Wasn't prepared for this cause
With the plate of misery in her hand,
So ghastly,

Sulked I felt

But crowned I was

Denial was my answer

But

She ran towards me

And I away,

But caught & entangled

I ate that all

After two,

Came she again

Spiteful already was

Thought optimistically as taught

But with the plate of melancholy in her hand,

Again I trod

She ran towards me

And I, as before, away

But entangled again

I ate that all

After three,

she came again

shaking as I already was

Just mustered up,

the result was all up

with the plate of grievances in her hand

this time

she ran towards me

and I stood still

she stopped and

metamorphosed it into

a plate of contented gold

amused

I ate it all

'Euphoria before time
Melancholia after some time,'
Is what I wanted,
Crowned I felt
When that crown I wore
Was her itself
What a servant
What a master
I bow before you
Destiny!

23. The Roads of Life

For some,
Thousands to stay together, but one for growing apart
Is enough to
Make multiple roads from one.

For some,
Thousands for growing apart, one to stay together
Is enough to
Make multiple roads one.

For some, encourage many from one.
For others, encourage many from one.
For I claim,
This prosperity lives the shortest
And
This unity lives the longest.

24. The Journey of a Soul

The alarm rang,
And here, my author sang
To me, a bidding goodbye,
For I had to now leave the sky

Entered the world
With joy's herald,
But a dismal to my expectations,
Here I was in some isolation.

A month or two
Did it take to
Realize the place where I was,
And then I took no pause.

Still, I cried,
Felt like I was being tied.
Darkness reigned everywhere,
But some voices ruled from somewhere.

After a month or eternity
Did I attain serenity.
Though my vision seemed defected,
My hearing wasn't affected.

Came the moment
When that place became scant,
For I was somewhat growing
And so was the space dwindling.

Saw some light,
For I opened my eyes in fright.
So soothingly, I cried,
For my results had finally arrived.

So beautiful, so enchanting,
Cast on me a spell captivating.
This world I waved to
Finally, to the humans, I said hello.

Years went by,
Extensively did I change and wry.
Lost my memory of my author,
For now, a human was my father.

Years and months passed,
This world tossed
Into a horrifying reality
Which now came into my destiny.

After some years again,
Did I finally set off for the gain?
A voyage of truth commenced,
The search for my existence inaugurated.

Months of search,
And years of scorch
Did I finally meet my author
And my real father.

Not for a second longer,
Was I to stay in this human world eager
For this frightful world was once my wish
But now, it was my last dish.

25. The Worthless Tears

The unique gift presented
By guest uninvited
Is still lurking
In my possession, unwilling.

When knocked on the door
By him who no one awaits,
The gift was presented
Along with duties destined.

In these racing times,
That gift costs endless dimes,
But had to be ceased
For there were duties predestined.

With locked doors

And no guests

Alone at last with the gift was I left.

The duties and responsibilities also fled.

When the door was alone left

By those grieves with injuries in the heart,

At last, the sigh wanted opened

The gift that was already dampened.

First by responsibilities predestined

Then by that gift vaporized

Those worthless tears in these times

Proved to be of endless dimes.

26. The Two Buttons of Our Face

Those two tiny buttons

On these tiny shirts

Were the last ones

To express.

But those in offer possession

Lay the foundation

Of our speech

And are the first ones to express and preach.

27. The Boon of Silence

Pleasant was the day,
And pouring like at the bay,
But here I was
Who wanted to scream at the topmost notch,
But whose answer was silence and the regular watch.

Confusion in the brain,
And silence in the vein,
Standing there, I was
Who had millions of feelings to express,
But whose answer was a blank silence to confess.

Adrenaline from the gland,
And inertia in my hand,
Sitting there, I was
Who was looking with despair,
But whose answer was silence quite unfair.

Pleasant will be the days to arrive,
With the promise to thrive,
And there I was
Who had a boon of silence,
Which was mistaken to be a bane of surfeit resilience.

28. The Journey

These moments of boredom,
Those fragments of the journey
Just adds a spice to your food
In the end, making nostalgic your mood.

This endless voyage will end.
Accompanied by an ultimate friend.
Your time comprised
Shall bring a smile wide.

Enjoy it till it lasts,
For then you will remember
The shadow it casts
Always on your soul when you remember.

29. Is Life Really A Race?

'Life Is a race
that you must embrace.'
told the one
who had in his life no one.

The wings gifted
fulfilled what I desired,
but then he again told
'life's a competition with hold.'

Presented before me
when I lost my glee,
Two sets of wings
to become a bird who sings.

The choice had to be made
whether the wings to compete
or those to complete
My perpetual desire
oh! I thought
this race is life,
but is that really life?

When the clock stroked
twelve, I fulfilled
my desire to touch the sky
and to fly high.

After a while,
I opened the humanity's file
kept in the sky
up above in the clouds high.

Fools are those
who live to compete
and live with conceit,
none other than imbecile humans are those.

Humanity teaches
and preaches
to not compete in life,
but to live your life.
It is what the file said
and I held my head,
went back and again, that imbecile said
'life is a competition withhold.'
amused I was
and laughed and laughed till alive I was.

30. I'll Forever Remember

Not a day passes by
Living the cunning life as a passerby
That I don't remember you
For my soul's only you.

The water the touches
my skin vouches,
The coming days to be a sweater
For I'll forevermore remember.

The dazzling rays of the Sun
That brings me fun
Conveys the days to be brighter
For I'll forevermore remember.

The icy cold chilling wind

That goes refined

Expresses the days to be finer

For I'll forevermore remember.

Finally, the fall

That appeals with a call

Embraces me to be happier

For I'll forevermore remember.

31. Memory

The beautiful morn
With a hilarious horn
Had marked the start
Of my life's cart.

The peals of laughter
With tears of joy, softer
Had with a sorrowful grave
Ended, did I not for happiness enough crave?

The wonderous fate
Put the plans on my plate.
To a halt, a ceaseless one,
For now, I found delight in not even one.

Tears shed and soured eyes.
Had crushed all the highs,
And presented the lowest of lows
For this was truly one of life's blows.

With laughter did she perish
Now I won't let her in only memories cherish,
For once, what held my breath
Now lies in a photograph without a single breath.

32. Proof to the Vices

Oh! Confused, a lad once said,
"The world is what it is not
And
The thoughts are what they prefer to be not."

The inclination of these troublemakers
Into making this world luxurious,
Sometimes make us forget
This world needs proof of our existence,
But not to the extent that we invite
The need to prove ourselves to our vices.

33. How the Tables Have Turned!

This desire I had
To go to a college abroad
Made me reminisce
Long before my departure.

A year before
Was there something rolling down my eyes,
Yes, they were those tears.
Today, instead of those fools,
They rolled who had, for times a thousand,
Made me a sore sobber.

Is it nostalgia
Which has struck me before time?
Because for sure, the ones whom I fought with
The words which fumed me with rage, unlimited
Are the ones which I now seek as I bid my adieu.

34. The Preserved Hearts

Thousands of times a day,
Does the time stop.
This power that I yield
Comes from you.

Whenever I see those moments
Together that we had spent,
That laughter, that fight and that unlimited teasing,
Does the time stop
Thousands of times a day.

The camera that once managed
To capture those moments
Some deleted, and some preserved.
I feel has now rusted, still
Thousands of times a day
Does the time stop.

Now that I think
At least I'm assured
Of someone who will hold my hands
If you'll let go of them,
Those millions of hearts preserved in
Thousands of our photographs together.

35. The Ignored Concern

Change is what I wanted,
Eager to take the next step is what I wished.
That happiness and delight
Washed away every fright.

But now have the tables turned,
Just the thought of being 18 turned,
What gave me a delight
Has turned into a heart-aching fright.

Rather to stay back is what I now want.
Rather to be a grown-up is now what haunts.
The watery eyes now yearn.
To get what was earlier ignored, a concern.

36. The Power of Silence

'Deep are the cuts I give.'
the knife proclaimed.
'Deeper are the injuries I give.'
The sword claimed.
'The wounds I give breaks hearts.'
The words proclaimed.

Well, 'is there even a comparison? '
The ignorance of the silence with pride claimed.

The Way of the World

1. The Fuelled Envy

It was the moon,
Rotten with envy
Who called for the comparison?
Between the two.

While the others knew
That both lay on the same plane
Yet not even a few,
But all said: the Sun is better than you.

2. Why Not Let Us Just Be?

Why do they say
That we should weigh
Our life, not as ours,
But as all of theirs?

Why do they want
That we shouldn't haunt
The people that surround
By treading the unventured ground.

Why are they so afraid,
For us not to be in the shade
And instead, to be out in the Sun
Making our lives a little fun.

Why? Why? Why?

Indeed, are protective.

The ones who are so active

Of our movements

But is it not about the moments?

Why? Why? Why?

Why not let us take chances?

Why not let us make mistakes?

Why not let us just be?

3. The Breeze

The breeze took me
On the voyage of the world
Less did I know
The world that awaits
Is not full of fairies
And not even full of scavengers,
But instead, full of those who are
From hearts hollowed and from minds witted.

4. The Confusion

What is this world?

Why is it so absurd?

How has it managed to be so deceitful?

Where is the world, once cheerful?

Who are the people with me?

Are they actually beside me?

Why are they so double-faced?

Where has their humanity ceased?

Who am I?

Why so lonely am I?

Despite being so surrounded?

Where has the real me vanished?

Why, amidst every life's sphere,

Am I left with a tear?

5. The Winged

You wish to fly high
Up In the sky
As that winged, you saw,
But why aren't you in awe,
For that creature
Represents a meaning deeper.

Propels to the sky
And also help others to fly high.
Not like us who wish to fly,
But want others to fall, why?

You call one love's symbol.
And the other doom's symbol
It's your hypocrisy,
But the birds have their own bureaucracy.

Have you ever seen their children,

For whom they have no vision?

They leave them to fly high,

As they wish, up in the sky,

But you bind the potion you brew

Why so, do you do?

6. The Deceit's Cunning Ploy

The boy who with worries
Clearly visible and disease
Grave was, without a doubt,
Rejected by 'The Deceit', no doubt.

But the boy, with a feigned smile
On his face while
Thousands of worries inside
Was by 'the deceit' not thrown outside,
But instead, with full arms welcomed
And in the deceit, those with welcomed
Who, like him, had a smile
To show while
A thousand problems inside
But not even a reflection outside.

7. Behind the Smile

With a smile, she laughed,

But with worry, I cried

Because I knew

that smile wasn't a favourable view.

No, I am not her woe,

But her friend, who has seen her sow

A thousand cries and words

Behind it to not show the world.

8. Where Does Our Childhood Go?

Yesterday, I met the world.
Who wanted the word
Out of a five-year-old
To be mature and bold.

Today, I again met that world.
With that child who had made his word
Mature enough, but the world said, 'Oh no!
Where did your childhood go?'

9. The One that is Ignored

Have you ever seen
In life, a hammer ever been
To the thought
That the branch valued not
Is now the ultimate tool
To cut that tree so cruel.

The one who is once ignored
And whose relation is soured
Might in the future
Yield the strength super
To catastrophically uproot
Your entire life's root.

10. Someone's Candle

No doubt, you must
Have come across the ones
Who remembers you just
When in peril, they are the ones.

And after you have solved
The problem they were in
By getting fully involved
They again forget, indeed, hurts within.

But have you ever thought,
'When do you need a candle?'
Yes, only when you ought
To fight the darkness you can't handle.

Just by this logic,
be happy and smile
Because you have the power symbolic
To make someone in peril smile.

11. A Breach in Humanity's Preach

Life is beautiful
Is what is comprehended.
But the question is
Should this be apprehended?
This definition makes frightful
The way death is apprehended.
But the question is
Should this be comprehended?
Isn't this a breach?
Isn't humanity's preach
Out of his reach?

From infancy to toddler
From puberty to senior
Knows all, only the ripened
Fruits of life
But the question is
Should this be perceived?
This definition makes staled
Rest of the fruits.
But the question is
Should this be conceived?
Isn't this a breach?
Isn't humanity's preach
Out of his reach?

Be it be revealed
The other's shore
Be it be concealed
Your entire ship's fore
This life is a euphoria
Is what is devised
But the question is
Should this be recognized?
This definition makes revealed
Your life's ship's fore,
To other's shore concealed.
The death's melancholia
Is what is recognized
But the question is
Should this be devised?
Isn't this a breach?
Isn't humanity's preach
Out of his reach?

12. The Sword

Friends were they,
A century ago.
Ages of friendship,
Centuries of trust,
Shattered in a day
By the curse of lust.

Rose the swords,
High up in the sky,
A futile war
With no one in the gain.
Called if off
With a wall.

Centuries of amity
Ripened into centuries of enmity.
What a disgrace!
But hey
Blind they were
With only a sight
And no vision.

Rose the swords
Time and again
With no winner
And no looser
With half weeping
And half moaning
left were only swords.

Once came a ruler,
A real ripened fruit of amity
With no enmity.
Enmity was his father's teaching,
But amity was his Thee's preaching.

Rose the swords,
Once again,
But for good.
Thee's preaching did he preach and
Melted the ice.
Taking lives did the swords know,
But for the first time
Did the swords mend lives.

13. The Reality of Today's World

Welcome! Welcome! Welcome!
To the world dropped in darkness.
The bearers of light were some,
Yet were the idols of kindness.
It was the past, not the present.

A dream broke,
And came forth today's horrific,
Horrific world
Where the igniters of light were deeply revered
But it was the world
Filled with the extinguishers
And it was the way of that world
That made them the igniters of light in
The eyes of the people
But far was the reality
And so was the luminosity.

14. The Definition

Filled with pride,
grasped with fear,
weak from the soul,
brave from body
Are what humans are.

Begging for respect,
craving for love,
lacking content,
abundant with greed
are how humans are.

Filled with happiness,
grasped with content,
agile from the body,
resolute from soul
are what humanity is.

Spreaders of respect,
granters of love,
lacking cupidity,
abundant with generosity
Are how humanity is

15. Home to House

Left out, I here stand,
Feeling as if everything's just a dune of sand.
Everything's mine,
Yet feels nothing's mine.
Family and friends all gone,
Here I stand all alone.

Left out, I here stand,
Feeling as if everything's just a dune of sand.
Time and again,
Have I heard and muted myself,
But the day,
I had to talk,
All went away and muted me again.

Left out, I here stand,

Feeling as if everything's just a dune of sand.

A time was when

All were united, but I was broken,

But now

All are broken, and I am again broken.

Left out, I here stand,

Feeling as if everything's just a dune of sand.

Just a sight ago,

Home was a home,

But now

Home is a big, isolated house.

16. A Congregation of Three

Despised was that pair
Of doves, in despair
Who on a hemlock tree
Sat in glee.

The best of friends
Who completed their ends
Were the three:
The two doves and the hemlock tree.

The doves were as pure as driven snow,
But the tree was as vicious as a crow.
Soon did, the time finally arrive
When the birds had to thrive.

Retained its purity,

One of the doves became the harbinger of serenity.

Distracted and clasped by the atrocity,

Another was trapped for perpetuity.

17. The Havoc

The war of thoughts
In our society
Prevail with full vigour,
Indeed, has in my life
Wreaked havoc.

Finally, by the day of the rise
Was the havoc wept,
As if were the tears
Swept from the face of
An innocent toddler.

18. Give Me Some Space

This world, oh! give me some space
To think and to act,
For it is not you but me who must lead my life.

This world, oh! give me some space
To process and to progress,
For now, I want the sovereign control
Of my mind and my actions.

19. The Right to Dream

Who are you
To question my existence?
You've taken enough,
Enough confidence
Have you snatched from me.

Always stood for peace,
But it ought not be my weakness.
Always burnt my dreams in that enormous flame,
But now, the river has changed its course.

Who are you
To question my existence?
You've snatched enough,
But today, I, a citizen of my dreams and hopes,
Forevermore, snatch this villainous right from you.

20. The Deceit of a Person

The path that you took,

So long ago

Has now left me with a choiceless choice.

I ask the woods of your existence,

But their answer

Has left me with sleepless nights.

The path you took

And the woods you passed,

Both are the witnesses

To your betrayal, not to me, but to your inner self.

21. The False Preachers

I've heard from the ones
Who preaches honesty
And yet, have reached only till its envy
That honesty with price comes.

But is it really so?
Wake up! It's a price that is not honest,
But the others have to pay till fullest.
Life's secrets so.

Thousands will say
What else can they do?
Maybe God knew
That honesty for others
Will always be sinners.
And those frail thousands can only say.

22. Maturity

The eyes of innocents
With loads of veracity sent
Shout out that life's a feel,
Not your wicked deal.

Well, the day everyone's happy.
Is unaware of the folly
That they commit with eyes wide open.
"Oh! My child is now mature." But broken
Is the soul
With a massive hole.

Maturity is the name.
That has the humans fame
Of the time of staging life as a deal
Instead of a soulful feel.

Friendship

1. The One Who Held My Hand

Well, like a wave
Once this naive person
Said hello to my dreams.
In my dreams,
He always resides
And I felt our tied lives.

Like a tsunami,
He wreaked havoc,
But like a surfer,
In my dreams,
We survived even those storms.

When I held his hand,
It felt like the world
I knew, was unknown,
And the world that everyone knew
Now knew me.

Soon the dream broke,
But unlike the rest,
He was with me,
Just not by my side.
He was within me as
He was none but
Just my CONFIDENCE
on my own self.

2. A True Friend

The imagination of someone
by my side in each one
of the highs and lows
I feel is in the hollows
of my heart
which has now fallen apart.

A friend, yes, is someone
easy to find, but the one
that is true for you
is not in this new world's tissue,
for now, the mind smirks at the silly
heart that feels deep agony
as it was from the very inception
the imagination of someone
the imagination of someone.

3. It is High Time

I held his hand
He promised and
Assured me never to let go,
But less did I know
The friendship was just
Till he got his benefits, so unjust!

Disheartened, I asked myself.
"In the battle, you have to fight yourself."
Is what someone replied.
It's not just him, indeed,
But the entire world,
Who is ready to be a part of my world,
Not for me, but for its own self.
Not for me, but for its own self.

Finally, I understood
This lesson stood
For my own rights
As enough of weeping all days and nights.
To hold, it was time
My own hand, it was high time!

4. The Seed of Words

They were your words, indeed,
That propelled me in need,
To get the required motivation
Even the night before my examination

They were also your words, indeed,
Who made me fall in need
When full of motivation
I sat in one of my life's examinations.

You know,
Your words not know
That they are the seeds
To the flowers or the weeds
That grow in my mind
But either case, no one seems to mind

5. The Real Friend

Close your eyes,

Think deep,

Recall your entire life

Your highs and your lows,

Your ups and your dips. Now,

Think Who your buddies are.

No one or someone?

Thank them.

Thank them twice.

Thank them as many times as you can.

Now,

Open your eyes and

try to find your buddies around you.

I bet the one you are looking for

ain't your real friend, but

just a passenger travelling on the same path

with the very same feeling as you are.

Ask yourself a small question,
"How often have you felt pain in your entire journey?"
Much frequently, yeah?
So, do you pay gratitude to it or just feel hurt or best ignore it?
Almost everyone carries it as a liability,
but mind you
Change in your perspective is the only need of the hour,
and you'll make it a rightful asset and a dear friend.

What is this pain?
Why do we feel pain?
What does it do?
Have you ever wondered?
But I bet you must have wondered what success is.

Let me tell you what they are.
Success is the ripened fruit of the hard work
of your everlasting friend, pain.
Pain makes you better.
But yeah, it's a foe of the fragile.
They will break and fail.

So, beware of it

If you are willed enough to pass his exam,

then no matter what, you'll achieve the summit of success with his help.

All pain wants to do is polish you into a diamond.

So, stop saying that no one's yours in this world

because this pain is always with you

To empower you.

Just change your perspective,

and your boat will easily sail through all the storms.

When those storms themselves are your besties.

6. Is there Even a Friend Around?

A crowd around, but is there even a friend surround?
Thousands to listen to,
but no one to talk to.

Around us is such a commotion.
Inside us is such a desolation.
Someone to approach, I await,
oh! In the crowd, I don't spot true friends that wait.

The true friends,
the desolation ends
are the commotion
that steal away the seclusion.

Oh! Finding that person
is difficult as a tone
but is that friend
really worth it all in the end?

Then stroke an idea
that changed my persona,
in the end,
I am forever my own dear friend.

7. Do I Really Need Them?

The ones who I really yearn for,
The ones who I really want to care for
Are the ones who make me question the following:
"Do I even need them in my life?"

Do I even need those friends?
Who shows to care,
But don't even have an iota?
Sometimes, the question is fade,
But sometimes, significant
As significant as my breath.

8. Befriend Yourself

To the winds, I recall
I once told to call
The ones who are
My friends, indeed.

Among that crowd
Was I in a delusional cloud
Because with the wind
Blew a mirror, only a mirror.

Well, it was the day.
And the wind's unique way,
To beware my inner self
Not to unfriend myself by only befriending others.

9. The Silence Between Friends

Fights and frights
Were much better
Than, these silencing days and nights
Which have made life an inch ruder.

The words which I used to
Fret over and ignore,
Now are pleaded to
Be heard, no matter were they sour.

Let's not end it like this,
Our friendship deserves better.
This ignorance and silence have left me in bits,
For once, let's forgo this societal pressure.

10. The Traveller Within

Sometimes this mind thinks
That travellers on this road
Will be a lot
Maybe some will get along
But will there be any?

Sometimes this heart feels.
The ones who have sprouted with me
Are the ones who will always walk with me
But will there be any?

All the time, I now believe.
That one traveller with a similar journey
Is the one that resides within
And he will always be.

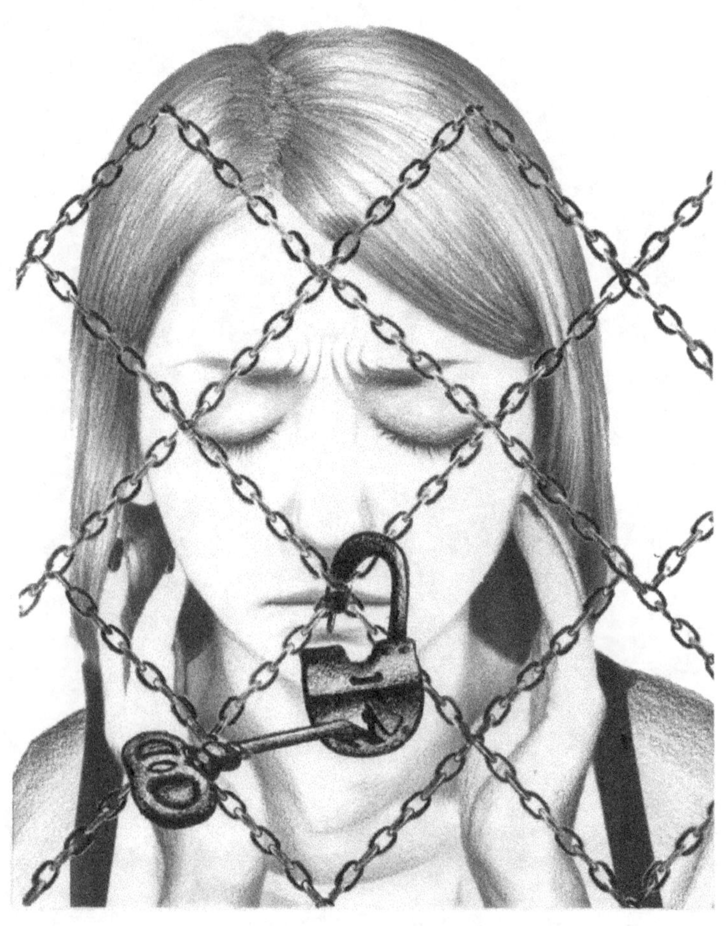

Reality and its Realisation

1. A Burden

Falling from the tree
Was the one leaf
That caught my eye,
But it was laden with grief.

Struck with realization
That is a burden if you become
Then your life's foundation,
Even your family, let's go to extent some.

2. The Insights of Mirror's Eyes

The brick walls that you've created
So stiff and strong do you appear
But for once, letting go is appreciated
Just let go of your fears.

Oh! Stop this pretence
I know what's going on inside of you
I know you are laughing and
I know your soul is crying.
Trust me, I know.

I make you see your reflection,
But even I have eyes
To look through you
And your trodden soul.

Just sit aside,
For once, let go of your tears.
For once, let go of your fears.
Just sit aside and
For once, let go.

3. The Final Assistance

Every time when my heart yearns.

And my head bows down in desire.

You remind it that it can get anything it wants.

A question arises.

Oh, my lord! Whether I'll find you by my side or not?

Every time my heart gets what it wants.

And my head bows down in gratitude.

You remind me that you have got me what I wanted.

A thought arises.

Oh, my lord! If it were just my efforts, I would never have what I have!

4. It Was You Who Held Me

After the hardest climb
I looked down
And asked myself,
Was it just me and my efforts?

No, this isn't self-doubt.
But 100% assurance
That my lord
It was you who held me
And that confidence, I say.

5. Our Word to Others

Sometimes

What we say, even a single time

Leads us to a hurricane

With loads of pain

Not because of what we said,

But because of what others think, we said.

6. Age's Folly

The world is the witness
To the stage
To which we confess
When we age.

Oh! But I have a doubt.
Why is it only with age
Do we realize in and out
That it is the great sage
Within us, in an unlocked cage
Who can make our life,
But if gripped in rage
Also has the power to break our life.

7. Conscious

Someone here is looking at the mirror
And consciously thinking about the need to be better.
Someone there is recording his voice
And consciously thinking to add some spice.

Well, to these gifts
Of imperfections, everyone shifts
Their attention is as if they are
Some pasts scare.

But surely come will time
When these will not be worth a dime
Instead, the marks of beauty
That defines one's personality.

8. Be Inspired

Calm your mind.
Broaden your eyes.
There's a lot around you
beyond your find.
The world's made to inspire.
Every single thing has something
to teach you,
and sets forth a quality
beneficial for you.
Every quality you want to inherit
is present around you.
Ready to aspire you.
Nothing is beyond the cult.
It's your perception that makes it difficult.

9. Open Your Eyes

Open your eyes and think bright.
You will be able to see what's right.
Life's far beyond fights and frights.
You must open your eyes to see the world's heights.

While opening your eyes,
You'll face the real world.
It's not only about you and your small little world.
The world's venturesome and
Trust me, once you come out of your shell,
You'll see that life's far beyond what you conceive it to be.

Open your eyes and think bright.
You will be able to see what's right.

10. Waken I Truly Had

Waken I had,
Felt like the day awaited me
for my voice to be heard.
The Sun shone brightly as though had shone never before,
For the creator and destroyer were waiting for me.

Waken I had,
Felt like the day awaited me
for my voice to be heard.
A sudden change of picturesque
And here I landed in his shadows.

Waken I had,
Felt like the day awaited me
for my voice to be heard.
Been waiting for this moment from the start,
So divine was the surrounding that
what I wished for was now deep down in the hell

and I was up in heaven.
Waken I had,
Felt like the day awaited me
for my voice to be heard.
My wishes were now buried in my mind's graveyard.
Promised me to fulfil all my wishes,
but there I was, such a fool
worshipped so hard, remembered him so much
not for the correct path,
but for some, wishes to be fulfilled.

Waken I had,
Felt like the day awaited me
for my voice to be heard.
Standing in his presence was all that mattered.
Got the answers to all my curious thoughts.
Got the answer to all my questions.
Got the answer to all my grievances.

Waken I had,
Felt like the day awaited me
for my voice to be heard.
He asked me my wishes time and again,

but there I was, lost in the unravelling clouds of happiness,
As though all the knowledge of this universe was on his face.
The need of that hour was the correct person
learned enough to be able to
see it,
read it,
grasp it,
and keep it with himself forever.

Waken I had,
Felt like the day awaited me
for my voice to be heard.
“How can I even wish for something?
I stand before you; I see you today,
but you see me every day.
I now see myself and my life from your perspective, not mine.
I was wrong to pray to you for worthless things.
Things that should have been my want.
Here I am apologizing for
making my need my want and
my want, my need.

Waken I had,
Felt like the day awaited me
for my voice to be heard.
You've given me such a picturesque life,

Blooming with flowers,
Glooming with stars,
how and why have I been keeping
the fruits aside and tasting the chillies.

Waken I had,
Felt like the day awaited me
for my voice to be heard.
The gifts of life I have are to be praised and lived with.
I see my family from here,
Protecting me like a shell,
and now I pledge to respect them,
Along with teaching all to respect them.

Don't you worry; this message of yours is mine to pass on
to everyone, be it a person who
blames his family for his failure

or

be it a person so successful in life

that he has forgotten who they are.

Waken I had,

Felt like the day awaited me

for my voice to be heard.

I don't think that I even have the right to

blame my fate for my failures and poverty,

For you have given me

a mind to think, to enlighten the world

Two hands to write, to make this world a better place

Two legs to walk, to explore this world

Two ears to listen, to grasp the knowledge for my life and my soul

Two eyes to see the happiness, to see the woes of this world

A mouth to speak, to tell this world a lot of things

What else could you have given me, my father!

Don't you worry; your message is mine to teach

the world how to see what we have.

Waken I had,

Felt like the day awaited me

for my voice to be heard.

One more truth is yes,

you have given me the freedom to think.
Now you have left it upon me to make myself
a soul dropped in darkness or a soul radiating light.

Don't you worry; I will imbibe in the world
'The very feeling of positivity.'

Waken I had,
Felt like the day awaited me
for my voice to be heard.
When I stepped back into my world,
I realized I was in my place and
what I had just experienced was
a conversation with the God within
Felt as if it was the day I truly woke up from my vicious sleep
For I pledged to tell the world that
Our family, our eyes, our ears,
our legs, our hands, our mouth, our mind
are thee's most precious gifts that we avail.
What should come first should always come first
And we shouldn't be mean enough to
line up our wishes before them.

11. Change: The Only Truth

Hanging out was what you preferred.

Sitting in is what I prefer.

Playing with friends was what you preferred.

Playing games on mobile is what I prefer.

Studying in school was what you preferred.

Studying at home is what I prefer.

Truth for you is not life for me.

Truth for me is new for you.

Change is what is the only truth.

12. A Contrasting Thought

What you say
Is what that matters.
What not matters most
is what your contrasting thought was.
A smile or a cry
Is yours to choose.

What you say
Is what that matters
What not matters most
is what your contrasting
Thoughts are,
Once said can't be undone
But
Once sought to undo the undone,
Everything can be done.

13. The Indelible Changes

The indelible changes

Are the only truth

That makes life solitude.

Inhumane or humane

Are yours to decide,

But they are not yours to decide.

14. The Light that Awaits

The bright sight
That awaits from eternity,
For your sight
To be placed with all serenity.

But lost, you are
In that vicious place,
For you are far
From your bright inner face.

15. The Light Outside

The flickering light

That on street

Glowed and

Extinguished

Made me realize

The needed eyes

To see the world outside

Are our insights inside.

16. Rising to the Stars

My longing
For you
Will be never-ending,
For I will always wait for you.

The stars in the sky
Ask my soul,
For they were up high
Dispelling light in darkness' soul.

The rise that I await
Will be the light
In the souls that wait,
For I seek our soul's light.

Darkness around us
Is what nighty night is.
Light in our souls
Is what the day is.

The stars that asked
Light the darkness around me.
The rise that is awaited
Lights the darkness in me.

17. The False Tomorrow's Sunrise

Tomorrow's sunrise is what I await,
For it is the hope for which I wait.
But will there be a new sunrise?
Or will the Sun never rise?

Tomorrow it is,
For which I dearly await.
Feeling enthusiastic or helpless.
Feeling rejuvenated or despaired.
Confused I am, perplexed I am

Today's the time,
Not tomorrow's sunrise.
Now is the time,
Not its next dime.

18. Salute to a Setting Sun?

The blazing light,
The rising Sun,
And his aspiration to be one
Was very common

Hands rose effortlessly
To salute the rising Sun.
Will his hands also rise
To salute the setting sun?

Told me not to fret,

But here I knew,

Rising Sun is what he aspired to be,

Maybe he will even be one.

But surety sustains its ground

In him is a setting sun

At last, during his last breath.

If not for himself or the world,

At least will have to kneel to thee.

My Real Desire

1. The Desire to be a Child

Sometimes,
You know
I just want to be!
I just want to be!
What I am!
Who I am!
And that is nothing, but
A child just.

But this world wants.
Well, there's a lot this world wants!
But you know what
I will be what I want
Free as a bird
And raw as a child.

2. What Does It Want?

It was that one fine day.
When I asked it not its way,
Its goal, or its intention,
But it is just one deep aspiration.

What I thought
Is not what it thought
Not about the future or the dollar,
Not even about being a scholar,
It just wanted to enjoy its life
And to actually live its life
Because it
Was none other than the real inner me.

3. Just a Step More

Just a step more
Is what I had asked,
But my life's sore
Now that my glee is masked.

Just a step more
Is what you had to take
With me, but you tore
Me, return, for God's sake.

Just a step more
Is what we desired,
But not long before
Over you, I mourned.

Just a step more
I had dared to ask.
Will just a step more
forevermore be an unfulfilled task.

4. The Myriad

What's your wish?

Your perpetual wish?

Oh! A man dressed in white and red,

once in a while asked.

My eyes lit up,

and my desires did lift,

for I had billions

of wishes and dreams in millions.

The moment came

to get fame,

but then he looked upon

and said no wishes from now on.

Quarrelled this muddle head,
For what he'd said,
return his words did he take,
for my myriad wishes weren't truly his take.

The Fierce

Stand

1. Wings of the Universe

I want to fly high,
saying discrimination goodbye.
Do not hold me down with the chains of prejudice.
Ideally, I should be with the crown,
but no, I am here somewhere, lost.

I want to fly high,
saying discrimination goodbye.
I am not the glass
which won't resist and will break.
I am a rock
which will defy when it's perceived to be a penny.

I want to fly high,
saying discrimination goodbye.
I am God's creation, not yours.
I have equal rights to become what I want.
I want to tell my successors who I am
How I have risen
What I achieved

I want to fly high, saying discrimination goodbye.
I want to fly high, saying discrimination goodbye.

2. Questions Arise

Are we your pets? Are we your puppets?
Are we your slaves? Are we the worst?
Questions arise
with answers as rare as diamond.
The united society says in one voice:
"This is normal, not a crime.
Hide, hide, never concede."
We control, we ignore,
but we're sorry:
It's our disagreement with your agreement.

Are we your pets? Are we your puppets?
Are we your slaves? Are we the worst?
Questions arise
with answers as rare as diamonds.
Now, they know not any age.
Even God's newly presented gift to his most preserved gift,
even the beginners and even the finishers,
All have to sacrifice themselves

because this world is no longer humane.
Are we your pets? Are we your puppets?
Are we your slaves? Are we the worst?
Questions arise
with answers as rare as diamonds.
Tens of thousands of reports
And many rendered unreported.
This is not a joke.
Brave enough to count but not brave enough to punish!

Are we your pets? Are we your puppets?
Are we your slaves? Are we the worst?
Questions arise
with answers as rare as diamonds.
Why are they born?
Just to exploit us!
We weep, we cry,
we suffer, we surrender.
They enjoy, and they last for long
with no fear and no guilt.

Are they going to make a better definition of humanity?
First, let them realize, let them see who they are
and then think of the world.
Are we your pets? Are we your puppets?
Are we your slaves? Are we the worst?
Questions arise
with answers as rare as diamonds.
We have united and with one voice,
We now say, "Be afraid of Kali; it is what we all can be.
Being a mother and a warrior is what we are,
Together we can, and we will
remove everything bad."
so, it's a message for you, the rapist.
'BEWARE OF WOMEN'

3. Our Freedom

Were we born to die?

Every day or forever!

And erase ourselves from the world.

We don't belong to you.

We belong to ourselves and our lord.

We will not say a word,

If he demands our life to compensate for a sin.

But father, who are you to punish us for what you have only given us-

OUR GENDER

Were we born to die?

Every day or forever!

We are born to fly.

Not to be locked up in a cell.

Why should we fear? Fear should the attacker, the acid attacker!

Why did you give us facial beauty, O' lord?

The beauty of our souls was enough for us.

Why do we have soft hearts, and they are so cruel?

Why don't we have the will to do an acid attack on others, and they do?

You are also no less.

Attacker attacked once, but you attack us 24*7.

They destroy our facial beauty, but you destroy our inner will.

This card of your cruelty won't be left unturned by us.

We now raise our voices and ask you

"Why aren't you ever exhausted, society?"

Were we born to die?

Every day or forever!

We are to be loved.

Not to be tied to the shackles of this society.

You brought us here

In this new house

So, don't we deserve freedom, respect, and equality?

Why do we have to go away from our loved ones?

And why not them?

Even accepted this, but then why do we get beaten up by them?
Why don't we have the audacity to do such an unjust crime?
And why are they proud to do it?
Why did you promise to fulfil all the requisites,
When you had to suppress me my entire life?
Think of yourself to be men, but let me tell you, our partners.
We ain't a burden on you, but you are a burden to society!

Were we born to die?
Every day or forever
We are born to rule.
We aren't your slaves.
Enough of being suppressed.
Enough of the following.
Now you all listen,
Here we are
united and unanimous
No longer shall we thrive.
No longer are we your slaves?

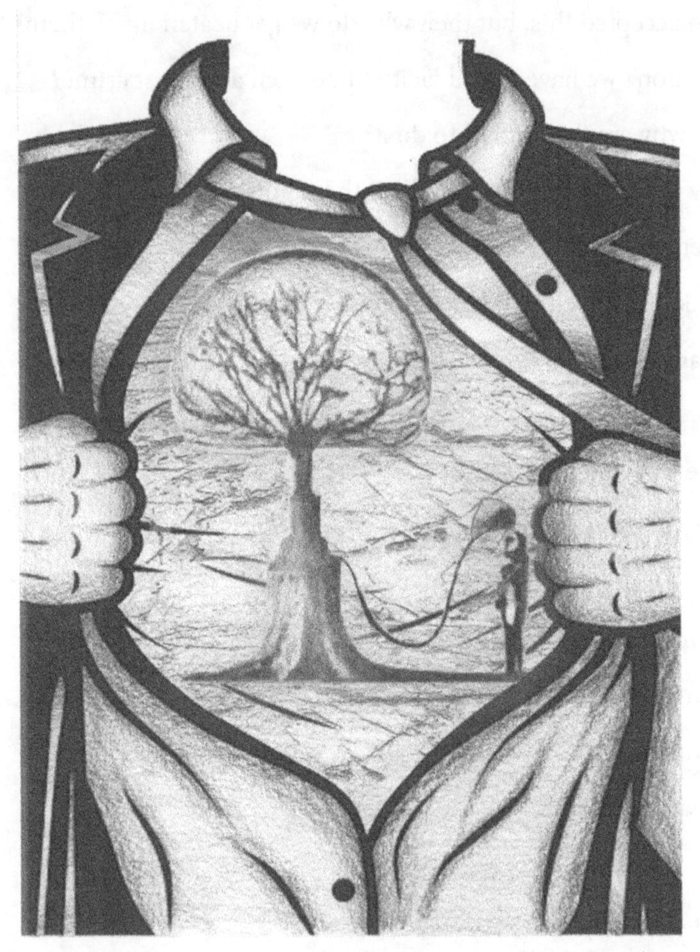

Nature and Technology

1. Mobiles: A Stigma in Society

A stain on society,
our old auxiliary
is now
our new adversary.

With no boundaries, no limits,
it is the most precious gem
without which no one's life is imaginable
and without which, the doors of our hearts for people around us will always be open.

Foundation of this new emerging tech-savvy world,
uprooting the lives of thousands,
this palm-sized gadget
is the one to be accused
for making all the relations glass delicate.

A looking companion,
but a house invader!
Stuck to everyone's palms forever,
Oh! My dear friends,
It's on us
to digest that this invention
has become
'A stigma on this society'.

2. The Tomorrow's Sunrise

Technology, Technology, Technology
is the future of tomorrow,
the basis of ecology,
and is the sunrise of tomorrow.

This backbone of the world
will become stronger and stronger.
Make it better,
You'll set the standards high
or else
You'll have to say the earth a bye!

It's said dreams are those which don't let you sleep,
But technology will help you sleep.
Technology, Technology, Technology
Is the future of tomorrow.

3. The Seldom Heard

Hear me!

Listen to me!

Hear what I am trying to tell you.

Listen to what I am dying to convey to you.

Oh, my children! Please hear me.

Please listen to my plea.

Please don't make me cry.

Please show mercy.

Please don't make me breathe my last.

Please forgive me.

Please don't ruin me.

Please understand,

Ruining me will ruin you.

Please, humans, my dearest children,

Don't axe your own feet.

Hear me!

Listen to me!

4. Covid: Nature's Ammunition

Father's alluring creation
always espied,
but seldom scrutinized.
Oh, my friend! nature
you are with me in grief
and absorb my pain.
You step behind me
and give me contentment's gain.
Just give me the sight
to see your plight.

Father's alluring creation
Always espied,
But seldom scrutinized.
Oh, my first teacher, nature
You tried to teach me.
You tried to warn me,

But see

The ones you taught

Have landed you distraught.

Just give me the adhesion

To explain my mates your COVID ammunition.

5. Feel the Nature

Feel the heat.
Let it heal.
Give it a treat.
Don't make a deal.

Feel the rain.
Let it fall.
Give it no pain
But make it a call.

Feel the breeze.
Let it whirl.
Give it a release.
Don't make it dismal.

6. The Drop's Voyage

The humans,
Oh! What shall I say?
First, their wonderful gift to the Ganges' sons
And then an awful surprise to say.

The happiness that we experienced
Lasted a while, for forevermore
We lay coughing, waiting to be asked
About our condition, nothing more.

Finally, coughing and sneezing,
we met my father
who was, in fever, shivering,
for I, in despair, then saw my brother.

Helpless, we stood,
and days went by,
For then, I woke up and stood
To see all the passersby.

Up high in the sky,
rising towards the cloud,
in the sky, I fly,
after the Sun's fury had peace found.

Held my brother's hand,
I floated above the lands.
Even the homeland and the sand,
For I only wanted to visit all the lands

Came the day when
my second home wept
by again those humans when
I was finally in delight; I also wept.

Falling from the sky,
did I reach the concrete,
for I was no longer up high.
It was just my fate's treat.

Those humans called me
and my brothers in a pipeline,
for travel thousands of miles, did we
after those taps, did humans open?

Oh! How silly they are!
My brothers and I in the sewage
were thrown, was that fair?
Is this such an age?

My brothers and I held hands,
for we had seen the fury
of the devil's lands,
I asked him to hurry.

That futile attempt
to save our lives
ended with my brother, who wept
as we said goodbye to all our lives.

The world that travelled
up to the north
had my mother and father despaired
and they stood and came forth.
The loss of their children beloved
is what no parent can endure,
for they stood united
to take revenge pure.

The race faced
My parents' unbridled fury
Who finally said
In a hurry.

The peace of our kind
has been ensured
by weeping your race unkind,
for our successors will be assured
of their survival on this planet
as the human scum will no longer be a part of the planet

The ones who don't value
our kind and our relations
will be given chances in thousands to the value
but their inability will end in their extinction

7. The Shocking Testimonial

"Oh! I express my gratitude."
Saying this, did I commit a mistake
To the drop that lay beside
Just waiting to fly high.

Hearing hysteric laughter,
Confused I thought
And finally mustered to add,
"Oh! The head bows down to you around whom my life revolves."

"Oh! I greet the pretence with a salute.
A drop of life or an ocean of death
Beware, I'm both."

That day, was the ice broken or my life's silence?
This shocked mind leaves it to his brothers and sisters
To decode this cypher facile.

We love creating beautiful books for you!

Come be a part of our ever-growing community of authors.
Grow, write, and publish with us!

Scan here to explore
books, authors and more

Connect with us on socials. We'd love to hear from you!

    Inkfeathers Publishing

www.ingramcontent.com/pod-product-compliance
Lightning Source LLC
LaVergne TN
LVHW012052160826
845678LV00014B/2803

* 9 7 8 8 1 1 9 4 8 3 0 6 8 *